THE SEVEN PRINCIPAL MUSICAL NOTES OF THE HINDUS,

WITH

THEIR PRESIDING DEITIES,

COMPOSED IN CELEBRATION OF THE BIRTH-DAY

OF

Her Most Gracious Majesty
THE EMPRESS OF INDIA,

BY

SANGÍTA-NÁYAKA

RAJAH SIR SOURINDRO MOHUN TAGORE, MUS. DOC.,

KNIGHT OF THE UNITED KINGDOM OF GREAT BRITAIN AND IRELAND;
COMPANION OF THE MOST EMINENT ORDER OF THE INDIAN EMPIRE;
KNIGHT GRAND CROSS, COMMANDER, OR CHEVALIER
OF VARIOUS IMPERIAL, ROYAL, OR REPUBLICAN ORDERS;
PROTECTOR, PRESIDENT, OR MEMBER OF VARIOUS LITERARY AND SCIENTIFIC SOCIETIES;
NAWAB OF THE PERSIAN EMPIRE;
&c., &c., &c.

LOW PRICE PUBLICATIONS
[A Division of D.K. Publishers Distributors (P) Ltd.]
Delhi-110052

Published by
Low Price Publications
A-6, Nimri Commercial Centre,
Near Ashok Vihar Phase-IV,
Delhi-110052
Phones: 27302453
e-mail: lpp@nde.vsnl.net.in
url: www.lppindia.com

First Published 1892

Reprinted in LPP 1990, 2006

Tagore, Sourindro Mohun (b. 1840 - d. 1914)

ISBN 81-7536-405-X

Printed at
D K Fine Art Press P Ltd.
Delhi-110052

PRINTED IN INDIA

To

The Hon'ble Sir Charles Alfred Elliott, K. C. S. I.,

&c., &c., &c.,

LIEUTENANT GOVERNOR OF BENGAL,

THIS BOOK

IS

WITH PERMISSION

MOST RESPECTFULLY DEDICATED

BY

HIS HONOR'S

MOST OBLIGED AND HUMBLE SERVANT,

S. M. TAGORE.

स्वरदेवाः ।

वह्निब्रह्मसरस्वत्यः शर्वश्रीशगणेश्वराः ।
सहस्रांशुरिति प्रोक्ताः क्रमात् षड्जादिदेवताः ॥

स्वरच्छन्दांसि ।

क्रमादनुष्टुप् गायत्री त्रिष्टुप् च बृहती ततः ।
पङ्क्तिरुष्णिक् च जगतीत्याहुश्छन्दांसि षादिषु ॥

TRANSLATION.

Agni, Brahmá, Sarasvatí, Vishṇu, Ganes'a, Mahádeva and Súryya are respectively said to be the presiding Deities of the Musical Notes—*Sharja, Rishabha, Gándhára, Madhyama, Panchama, Dhaivata* and *Nisháda.* To these notes belong the respective poetical metres, *Anushtup, Gáyattrí, Trishtup, Brihati, Paṅkti, Ushṇik* and *Jagati.*

भारतीयसङ्गीतदत्तमहाराज्ञीभिक्टोरियाकल्याणवादः।

यस्मिन् भारतभूमिभर्त्तुरमले सिंहासने संस्थिता
भिवेऽरौ समदर्शिताप्रभृतिभिः श्रेष्ठैर्गुणैर्भूषिता।
ज्ञानाढ्या वयसा वृद्धा प्रकृतिभिः संस्तूयमाना च सा
अस्माकं हितकारिणी मतिमती भिक्टोरिया पातु नः ॥ १ ॥

शिष्टानां प्रतिपालिका सकरुणा मातानुरूपा सदा
दुष्टानां शमनोपमा ह्यकरुणा शास्त्री प्रतापान्विता।
गान्धर्व्वे रसिका परा सुविमले काव्ये च धीरप्रिये
अस्माकं हितकारिणी मतिमती भिक्टोरिया पातु नः ॥ २ ॥

यस्या धार्म्मिकतां तथा विनयितां कार्य्ये निजे दक्षतां
औदार्य्यं मनुजोत्तरं सुविदुषां सम्मानने स्वाग्रहं।
स्मृत्वा नो हृदिकन्दरेऽनुपममुद्वारांनिधिर्वर्द्धते
अस्माकं हितकारिणी मतिमती भिक्टोरिया पातु नः ॥ ३ ॥

जीव त्वं शिवमस्तु ते ननु महाभागे स्वधाभोजिनो
ब्रह्मोपेन्द्रमहेश्वरप्रभृतयो देवा दिशामीश्वराः।
आदित्यादिनवग्रहा वसुगणाः साध्यास्तथा किन्नराः
कल्याणं सुखसाधनं तव सदा कुर्व्वन्तु मातर्मुदा ॥ ४ ॥

Indian Music's Address

TO

EMPRESS VICTORIA.

TRANSLATION.

(1)

MAY She Who graces now the Indian Throne, Who looks upon friend and foe with an equal eye, Who is adorned with the highest virtues, Who is full of knowledge and wisdom, Who is our greatest Benefactress, and Who is adored by Her subjects in mind and by word—May Victoria protect us all !

(2)

May She, Who cherishes the good like a benign Mother, Who chastises the wicked like the implacable Destroyer, Who is possessed of majesty, wisdom and benevolent feelings, Who is the Patroness of Music, Poetry and other Fine Arts—May Victoria protect us all !

(3)

May She, the thought of whose righteousness, affability, attention to duty, transcendental magnanimity, and readiness to honor learning, causes the ocean of unutterable joy to overflow the heart—May the gifted and benevolent Victoria protect us all !

(4)

Mayst Thou, O luckiest of the lucky ! live long and in prosperity ! May Brahmá, Vishnu, Síva, and other deities,—may the *Pitris,* may Indra and other regents of the quarters of the Universe —may the Sun and other planets, may the eight *Vasus,* the *Sádhyas, Kinnaras,* and other demi-gods shower blessings on Thee !

देवीं काव्यविधायिनीं गुणमयीं सङ्गीतहर्षप्रदा
देवी नस्तव जन्मवासरदिनं ज्ञात्वागतं साम्प्रतं ।
भूत्वा स्वां रुचिरामनन्यहृदया धृत्वा करे कच्छपीं
हृष्टा पङ्कजलोचनाममलमती संबुध्य सम्भाषते ॥ ५ ॥

आवां या परितृप्यति प्रकृतिभिः शश्वत् स्वकीयैर्गुणै
राज्ञ्याशीर्व्वचनावलीं रचय हे तस्या हि काव्यानगे ।
श्लाघ्यां तामुपवीणयामि सततं काव्याधिदेवी वरा
उक्तेत्थं विमलाख्यया सकृपया सङ्गीतदेव्या तदा ॥ ६ ॥

सङ्गीतस्वरदेवताश्रितवतीं तत्तत्स्वरच्छन्दसा
आशीर्व्वादविधायिनीं रचयति स्वाद्वीं हृदाह्लादिनीं ।
गाथां रागलयाश्रयां सुमधुरं गीतेश्वरी गायति
राजत्वे तव भारते विघटितं यद्द यत् सुखं पश्य तत् ॥ ७ ॥

युग्मकम्

(5)

O Mother Victoria! Knowing that the anniversary of Thy Birth-day was drawing nigh, the Goddess of Music, whose eyes are lotus-like and whose heart is marble-pure, took up the charming *Kachchhapi Víná* in her hands, and with a joyful heart and in rapturous tones, addressed the Goddess of Poetry thus :—

(6, 7)

"O Goddess of Poetry! Compose some benedictory verses on behalf of that mighty Empress Who has captivated the hearts of Her subjects by Her manifold virtues, and I shall sing them to the accompaniment of the Víná." Accosted thus, the Goddess of Poetry invoked the aid of the deities who preside over the Seven Musical Notes, and with the help of the metre that appertains to each, and the soul-entrancing melodies and measures, composed some strains which the Goddess of Music began to sing, scattering sweetness all around.

And thus pleasure and joy pervade Thy blessed Empire!

काव्याधिदेवीमूर्त्तिस्तु ।

तरुणशकलमिन्दोर्विभ्रती शुभ्रकान्तिः
कुचभरनमिताङ्गी सन्निषण्णा सिताब्जे ।
निजकरकमलोद्यल्लेखनीपुस्तकश्रीः
सकलविभवसिद्ध्यै पातु वाग्देवता नः ॥

सङ्गीताधिदेवीमूर्त्तिस्तु ।

या कुन्देन्दुतुषारहारधवला या श्वेतपद्मासना
या वीणावरदण्डमण्डितभुजा या शुभ्रवस्त्रावृता ।
या ब्रह्माच्युतशङ्करप्रभृतिभिर्देवैः सदा वन्दिता
सा मां पातु सरस्वती भगवती निःशेषजाड्यापहा ॥

षड्जाधिदेवः अग्निः ।

१

अनुष्टुप्छन्दसा ।

पिशङ्गश्मश्रुकेशाक्षः स्थूलाङ्गजठरोऽरुणः ।
अजारूढः साक्षमालः सप्तार्चिः शक्तिधारकः ॥

षड्जाधिपोऽनलो नित्यं तृणादौ स्वं कलेवरं ।
यथा वर्द्धयते श्रीमान् पवित्रीकुरुते जगत् ॥

तथाऽरिहते प्रतापाग्निं स्वपक्षे च पवित्रतां ।
विदधातु महातेजा मातर्भिक्टोरिये तव ॥

विशेषकम् ।

I.

Agni,

The Presiding Deity of Sharja. (C.)

TRANSLATION.

O Noble Empress! Who art interested in the welfare of others, may Agni, who is seated on a goat, whose robust body shines with crimson hue, and whose face is adorned with violet eyes and with a brown beard, and who bears a head of tawny hair, and wears sacred beads of "Rudráksha" round his neck—May the all-powerful Agni, the presiding Deity of "Sharja," radiant with seven resplendent rays, and holding in his hand the "Śakti"—the weapon of might—destroy thy enemies, even as he consumes straws by his all-consuming flame, and add to thy holiness, even as he consecrates the world by his hallowed touch!

KALYÁṈA.

TÁLA—CHAUTÁLA.

First Strain.

Second Strain.

Third Strain.

ऋषभाधिदेवः ब्रह्मा ।

२

गायत्रीछन्दसा ।

चतुर्वक्त्रशोभी चतुर्वाहुशाली ।
असृग्वर्णदेहो मरालाधिरूढ़: ॥

उमेशाक्षमाली सदा वेदगायी ।
सुरेन्द्रेण सेव्यो विधिर्विश्वकर्त्ता ॥

द्वितीयस्वरस्याधिपोऽयं प्रसन्नः ।
सदा ते करोतु प्रजावृद्धिमार्य्ये ॥

विशेषकम् ।

II.

Brahma,

The Presiding Deity of Rishabha. *(D.)*

TRANSLATION.

O Noble Victoria! May Bráhma, who is adorned with four faces and with four arms, seated on a swan, and decked with a string of sacred "Rudráksha," and who always chants the "Vedas," and is revered by Indra, the Prince of Gods—May Brahma, the Creator of the Universe, the presiding Deity of "Rishava," favorably inclined towards thee, bless Thee and Thine!

SURATA.

Tála—SURPHÁKTÁ.

First Strain.

Second Strain.

Third Strain.

गान्धाराधिदेवी सरस्वती।

२

त्रिष्टुप्छन्दसा।

श्वेताब्जवासा सितवस्त्रभूषा
श्वेताङ्गयष्टिः सितवज्रहारा।
स्मेरानना कोटिसुधांशुभासा
देवैः सदा पूजितपादपद्मा॥

अज्ञानताध्वान्तविनाशदीपः
प्रज्ञाखरांशूदयगोत्ररूपा।
सम्मानकुल्याभरकल्पवृष्टिः
साम्राज्यसौख्याधिकसौख्यदात्री॥

वाग्देवता विश्वजनानुसेव्या
गान्धारदेवी नियतं प्रसन्ना।
आभातु शश्वत्तव कण्ठलग्ना
भिक्टोरिये त्वां न जहात जातु॥

विशेषकम्।

III.

Sarasvati,

The Presiding Deity of Gándhára. *(E.)*

TRANSLATION.

O Noble Mother! May Sarasvati, who is seated on a white lotus, whose body gleams with silvery hue, and whose face, with a serene smile; who is clad in white, who wears a gemmed necklace of virgin lustre, who is effulgent like myriads of moons, and whose lotus-feet are worshipped by the Gods—

Sarasvati, who diffuses a dawn of reason over the mind, and is the source of light that chases away ignorance, and whose favorable glance pours a flood of honor on her favored sons, even as a water-fall, its torrent of water; and who grants them felicity, worth more than an empire—

May Sarasvati—an object of universal veneration—the presiding Deity of "Gándhára," O Victoria!—ever grace Thy throat, nor leave Thy blessed company even in forgetfulness!

JHIJHITI.

TÁLA—JHÁÑPTÁLA.

First Strain.

Second Strain.

Third Strain.

मध्यमस्वराधिदेवः महादेवः ।

४

बृहतीच्छन्दसा ।

सितशैलशुभ्रदेहधृक्
कुमुदेशमौलिभूषणः ।
मृगशत्रुचर्म्मशाटको
मणिभूषणाढ्यविग्रहः ॥

नलिनासनः स्तुतोऽमरैः
भवभीतिहारकः परः ।
खलु मध्यमस्वराधिपो
गिरिजापतिः शुभङ्करः ॥

अनुकम्पया निरन्तरं
अशुभं करोतु निष्कृतं ।
विदधातु ते शिवं प्रसु
इति याच्यते मयाधुना ॥

विशेषकम् ।

IV.

Mahádeva,

The Presiding Deity of Madhyama. (F.)

TRANSLATION.

O Illustrious Empress! May Mahádeva, who is vested in tiger-skin, whose body is adorned with flashing gems and effulgent like the snow-clad Himalaya, and whose forehead shines with the crescent moon—

Mahádeva, the consort of the daughter of the Mountain-king, who is seated on a lotus, and whose praises are sung by the Gods—May that Divine Being, the presiding Deity of "Madhyama," the remover of the fears of mortality, and the source of all blessings, in mercy, O Noble Victoria, remove all thy evils!

KEDÁRÁ.

TÁLA—EKATÁLÁ.

First Strain.

Second Strain.

Third Strain.

पञ्चमाधिदेवः विष्णुः ।

५

पङ्क्तिच्छन्दसा ।

सवितृमण्डलस्थपूरुषः
कनककुण्डलान्वितः परः ।
सरसिजासनोपरिस्थितो-
ऽङ्गदविभूषितो रमापतिः ॥

विमलशङ्खचक्रधारको
मुकुटशोभितोत्तमाङ्गकः ।
विधृतरत्नहारराजितो
रुचिरशातकुम्भविग्रहः ॥

ललितपञ्चमस्वराधिपो
भुवनपालको जगत्प्रभुः ।
मुररिपुर्निरन्तरं स्वयं
जननि पातु वः सदा मुदा ॥

विशेषकम् ।

V.

Vishnu,

The Presiding Deity of Panchama. (G.)

TRANSLATION.

O Benign Mother! May that being, of form beautiful and sublime, Vishnu,—the lord of Lakshmí, enshrined on a lotus in the solar region, with a crown on his forehead,—his body shining with golden lustre, his ears adorned with golden rings and his arms, with bracelets,—holding in his hands the sacred conch and discus and wearing a necklace, flashing with gems of rare brilliance,—May Vishnu, who is the presiding Deity of mellow "Panchama," who is the slayer of the mighty demon, Mura, and who is the cherisher of the world, protect Thee!

BIBHÁSA.

TÁLA—ÁRÁ-CHAUTÁLA.

First Strain.

Second Strain.

Third Strain.

धैवताधिदेव: गणेश: ।

६

उष्णिक्छन्दसा ।

खर्व्व: स्थूलशरीरो नागेन्द्रास्यमनोज्ञ: ।
प्रस्यन्दन्मदगन्धभ्रान्ताल्याकुलगण्ड: ॥

दन्ताघातविदीर्णद्विड्रक्तारुणगात्र: ।
उत्तुङ्गोदरशोभो वाञ्छासिद्धिकरोऽसौ ॥

सर्व्वां धैवतदेवो वाञ्छामाशु शुभां ते ।
विघ्नेशो हृदयस्थां सम्पूर्णां प्रकरोतु ॥

विशेषकम् ।

VI.

Gaṇeśa,

The Presiding Deity of Dhaibata. (A.)

TRANSLATION.

O Mighty Empress! May the gorbellied, elephant-faced Ganeśa, about whose temples bees are roving, intoxicated by the smell of the juice flowing from them, and whose handsome body of a small stature is besmeared with the blood of the enemy, stabbed by his tusks,—May Ganeśa, the presiding Deity of "Dhaibata," the source of all blessings and the bestower of all success, accomplish Thy desires!

KHÁMBÁBATÍ.

TÁLA—MADHYAMÁNA.

First Strain.

Second Strain.

Third Strain.

निषादाधिदेवः सूर्यः ।

७

जगतीच्छन्दसा ।

रक्ताम्बुजन्मासन उष्णदीधितिः
पद्मद्वयाभीतिवरान् दधत् करैः ।
माणिक्यमौलिः क्षतजाङ्गदीप्तिधृक्
दीप्तत्रिनेत्रो जगतामधीश्वरः ॥

आत्मा प्रजानां गतिरादिकारणं
चक्षुश्च सेव्यः परमार्थदर्शिभिः ।
भानुर्निषादस्वरदेवता सदा
आरोग्यमायुर्विदधातु ते सदा ॥

युग्मकम् ।

VII.

Suryya,

The Presiding Deity of Nisháda. (B.)

TRANSLATION.

O Noble Mother! May Suryya,—enthroned on a ruby lotus, adorned with four hands: two, graced with lilies, and of the other two, one holding out the boon, and the other, the promise of safety,—gleaming with glowing eyes and with a crown on his forehead, flaming with resplendent rubies,—radiant with powerful rays and beaming with blood-red effulgence—May the Sun, the presiding Deity of "Nisháda," the original cause of the universe, the source of life and light, and the spring of salvation, grant Thee, Empress Victoria, health and long life!

BEHÁGA.

TÁLA—KÁOYÁLÍ.

First Strain.

Second Strain.

सङ्गीतकाव्यामृतसिन्धुदेवी-
संप्राथ्यमानाः स्वरसप्तदेवाः ।
आशीर्व्विधानं तव कल्याणार्थं
कुर्व्वन्ति तौर्य्यत्रिककाव्यशाखा ॥ १ ॥

लक्ष्मीः सुचञ्चमतिः सततं गृहे ते
खञ्जा सुखं निवसतु स्वपुरं विहाय ।
तज्जीवनं भवतु मानुषजीवकाल-
व्यापि प्रसन्नहृदया विहर स्ववर्गैः ॥ २ ॥

जय जय जननि त्वं हृत्स्थसर्व्वैपसितेऽर्थै
कुरु कुरु जनचित्तं मोदितं सर्व्वकृत्यैः ।
हर हर परदुःखं वाङ्मनःकायकार्य्यैः
चर चर दुरलभ्यामुन्नतिं मर्त्त्यवृन्दैः ॥ ३ ॥

समाप्तोऽयं ग्रन्थः ।

TRANSLATION.

(1)

THUS invoked by the Powers of the nectareous deep of music and verse, the seven presiding Deities of the Musical Notes join, O Benign Mother, in pronouncing the following benedictions for Thy well-being :—

(2)

"May Lakshmí, the Goddess of Fortune, fickle as she is, quit her heavenly mansion, and being crippled, O Mother, ever abide with Thee ! Mayst Thou live a long life, and pass Thy days cheerfully in the sweet company of Thy dear relatives !

(3)

"O Gracious Mother ! May success attend Thee in all Thy pursuits, and victory and popularity be Thine ! Remove the sorrows of others with all Thy might, and continue to remain, O Mighty Empress, at the pinnacle of power and prosperity, inaccessible to an ordinary earthly being !"

THE END.

Printed by I. C. Bose & Co., Stanhope Press, 249, Bow-Bazar Street, Calcutta.